Contents

Written by Lisa Regan
Illustrated by Angelika Scudamore

First published 2016 by Brown Watson
The Old Mill, 76 Fleckney Road
Kibworth Beauchamp
Leicestershire LE8 0HG

ISBN: 978 0 7097 2308 0
© 2016 Brown Watson, England
Reprinted 2016, 2018
Printed in Malaysia

Now I Can

READ
Farm Stories

Brown Watson

ENGLAND

Little Lost Lamb

Once upon a time, there was
a little lamb named Barnaby.
He was the smallest lamb of
them all. He couldn't even reach
the flowers to nibble on their
tasty petals.

Gradually, though, Barnaby
got bigger. He drank his
mummy's milk, and he grew and
grew. The big sheep laughed
to see him run and leap in the
meadow, eating whatever
he could find.

One day, Barnaby jumped through a hole in the fence, and trotted towards the cornfield across the lane. 'Now I am big enough to explore on my own!' he said, stretching his long legs.

However, Barnaby was not as tall as he needed to be. The corn had grown, too, and reached high over his head. 'Help!' he bleated. 'Come and find me! This corn is way too tall for me to see!'

Luckily, Sammy the Shire horse
was grazing nearby. Even her
long legs were partly covered by
the corn. Sammy plodded over
to Barnaby and nudged him
in the right direction.

He trotted blindly through
the giant stalks and found his
mummy waiting for him at the
edge. 'Thank you, Sammy,'
she said. 'And as for you, little
Barnaby – perhaps you're not
as big as you think you are!'

Read these words again

across	reach
petals	tasty
lamb	enough
meadow	covered
eating	through
perhaps	blindly
grown	direction

What can you see here?

flowers

tree

horse

lamb

corn

poppy

Crossing the River

One day, a cat, a donkey, and a duck were out walking. The farmer was at the market, so they could do what they wanted all day long. The sun was shining and the birds were singing.

As they wandered away from the farm, they came to a river. It was flowing fast, and the water looked very deep. On the other side of the river lay a sunny glade, perfect for an afternoon nap.

The animals looked at each other. 'It is too deep for us to wade across,' said the donkey. 'I'm going to walk further up the bank to find a bridge.'

The cat agreed. 'It is too fast and frightening for me,' he meowed. 'I don't want to get my paws wet.' So they set off along the riverbank, and walked for miles and miles to find a bridge.

As the cat and the donkey huffed and puffed in the heat of the sun, they suddenly wondered where the duck had gone. His little legs didn't carry him very fast, and he must have been left behind.

When the pair eventually arrived at the sunny glade, they were astonished to find the duck there already. 'But how...?' they gasped. 'I'm a duck, silly,' he quacked. 'How do you think I got across?'

Read these words again

silly

river

market

glade

perfect

donkey

flowing

afternoon

suddenly

already

shining

singing

bridge

astonished

What can you see here?

butterfly

duck

bridge

donkey

river

cat

21

When Tilly went to Town

All the animals on the farm
were excited. It was market day,
and they wondered whose turn it
would be to ride in the trailer
behind Farmer John's tractor.

Tilly the Turkey was the only
animal that didn't want to go.
She was scared that Farmer John
might sell her, and she would
never see her farmyard
friends again.

Farmer John put on his jacket
and walked out into the yard.
He picked up Tilly, tucked her
under his arm, and gently
placed her in his trailer.
'Don't worry, Tilly,' he said.
'It will be fun!'

As they arrived at the
market place, Tilly got even
more scared. She flew out of
the trailer and hid behind some
fruit. Farmer John found her,
and carried her back to his stall.

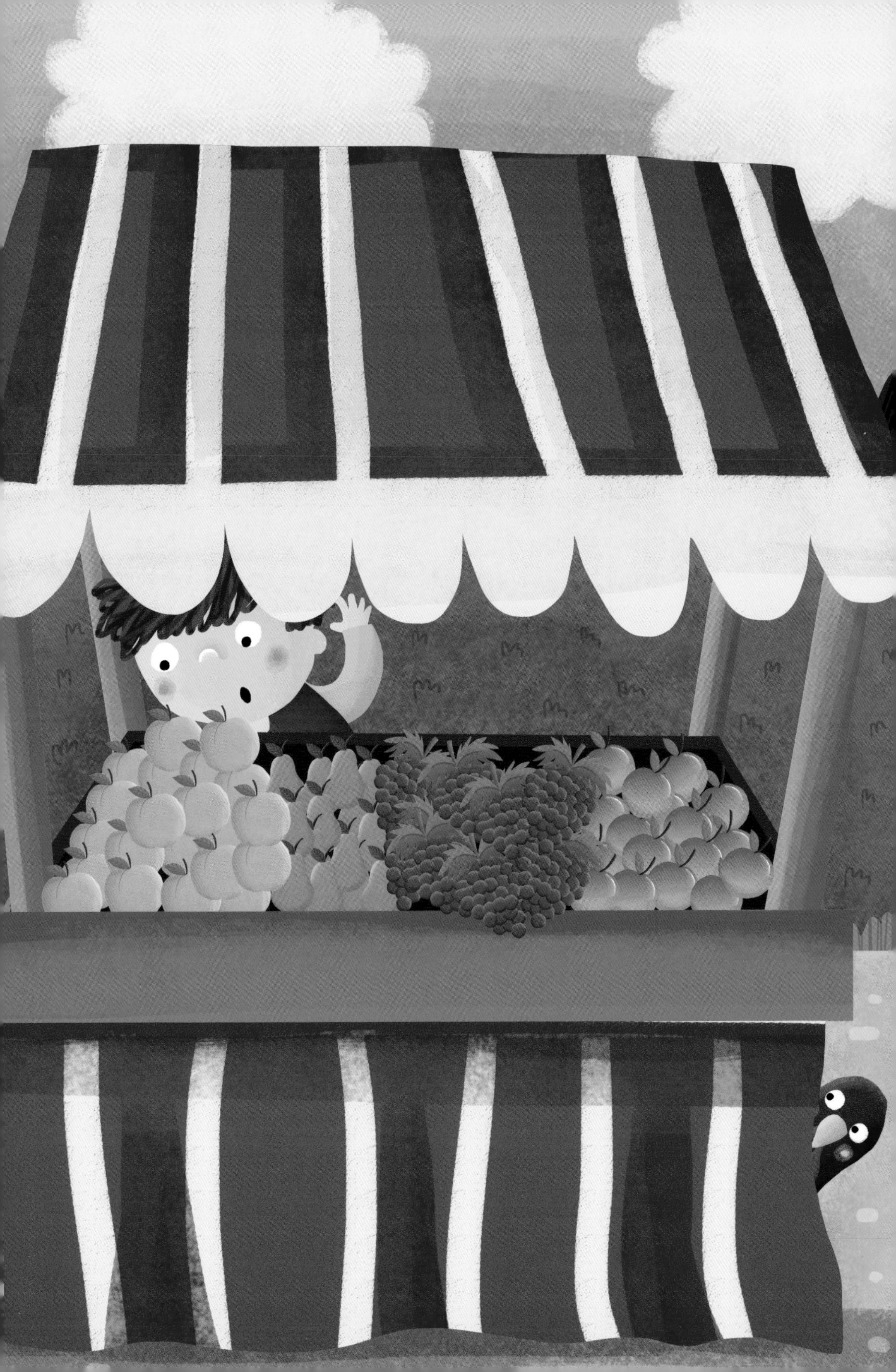

When Tilly arrived home that night, she was tired but happy. Her friends all gathered around to hear about her day. Tilly proudly told them all about it.

Farmer John had entered her into a competition, and she had won first prize! All the judges thought she was the finest turkey they had ever seen. Now she never hides from Farmer John on market day!

Read these words again

fruit	judges
hides	tucked
whose	trailer
under	carried
behind	proudly
scared	excited
finest	friends

fruit

farm cat

cow

turkey

hen

rosette

Trundles the Tractor

Trundles lived in a barn, with lots of farm mice that slept under his bonnet. Every morning, Trundles went to work with Farmer Stan, and the mice ran outside to play.

One day, the mice ran down the lane, and came to a sudden halt. In front of them was an enormous puddle, as large as a lake. 'Quick, quick!' they squeaked. 'We must warn Trundles!'

The little mice ran into the yard.
The only creature there was the
cat, curled up in a patch of
sunshine. They were afraid to
ask if she had seen Trundles
recently. But this was an
emergency situation!

The cat yawned and stretched,
and opened one eye. 'Yes,' she
said, 'I heard Trundles just now.
He was driving down the lane
with Farmer Stan.' The mice
squealed in dismay. 'He will
fall in the lake!'

Quickly, the mice scampered along the wall and under the fence. 'Stop!' they shouted. 'Trundles, stop! You will fall down the hole!' But Trundles' engine was too noisy and he couldn't hear.

The mice watched anxiously as Trundles drove towards the hole. But of course, his wheels were tall and his tyres were chunky, and he splashed through easily. That's what tractors are made for!

Read these words again

barn   bonnet

fence   sunshine

warn   dismay

morning engine

yawned easily

afraid   tyres

puddle   patch

What can you see here?

window

puddle

pebbles

mice

bucket

ladder

37

The Sheep who Came in from the Cold

Lacey the sheep was a wanderer. She wandered freely around the farm, saying hello to all the other animals. Every evening, she wandered past the farmhouse, and looked inside.

A warm glow spread from the farmhouse windows, and it looked so inviting. Lacey wished she could wander inside and curl up by the fire. She could keep the children company!

One night, as Lacey went wandering, the farmhouse door opened. The farmer walked across to the woodshed, leaving the door open slightly while he was gone. Lacey seized her chance.

She trotted across to the doorstep, and nudged the door open a little wider. Then she slipped inside and looked around. It was so warm and cosy! She trotted towards the fire and climbed on the sofa.

The next thing Lacey knew,
she was being prodded and poked.
What was happening? She could
feel bony elbows in her sides, and
little fingers curled into her wool.
She opened her eyes.

Lacey realised she had fallen
asleep in the warmth from the fire.
The farmer's children snuggled up
next to her and begged for her to
stay indoors. She was so cuddly
and warm!

Read these words again

wander	cuddly
asleep	warmth
chance	doorstep
elbows	night
around	spread
inside	seized
company	inviting

What can you see here?

bookshelf

picture

plants

sheep

rug

window

45

Little Chick's Big Adventure

Little Chick pecked at the corn on the ground. 'I wonder what the world looks like?' she said to herself. So she asked Granny Hen. 'I'll show you,' said Granny, and Little Chick hopped on her back.

Granny Hen strode to the edge of the yard, and flew up onto the fence. Little Chick looked at the stables stretching beyond. 'Wow!' she chirped. 'It's so big!'

Just then, Suki Sheepdog
walked past. 'It's even bigger
than that,' she barked. 'Hop on,
I'll show you.' So Little Chick
jumped off the fence and onto
Suki's furry back.

Suki ran past the stables and
out of the gate. She trotted
down the lane and stopped at
the wall. Little Chick looked at
the fields stretching beyond.
'Wow!' she chirped.
'It's enormous!'

Pippa Pony cantered over to see them. 'It's even bigger than that,' she whinnied. 'Hop on, I'll show you.' Little Chick clambered nervously up onto Pippa's back.

Pippa galloped across the field and stopped at the trees. Little Chick looked into the dark woods and gulped. 'It's too big!' she stammered. 'Please can I go home now?'

Read these words again

looked ground
stables edge
fence beyond
barked stopped
please field
furry nervously
world enormous

What can you see here?

tree

scarecrow

fence

dog

horse

forest

53

The Very Helpful Tractor

Tiny the Tractor loved to be useful. He wanted to help wherever he could. But he was very small. There were many jobs on the farm that were just too big for him.

Tony the Tractor did most of the work. He pulled the plough that dug up the fields every year. Tiny could only watch from the edge, and pull up a few weeds.

Tony also pulled the machine to spread manure where the crops were growing. 'You don't want to do this job,' he chuffed. 'It's very smelly!' But Tiny did. He just wanted to help.

Once the crops were harvested and the straw was all gathered into bales, Tony drove around the fields collecting them into one place. His trailer was piled high with large, heavy bales.

Tiny trundled along behind,
raking up any leftover strands.
Then he heard a thump and a
bang, and Tony stopped.
He had a puncture!

Finally, Tiny knew he could help.
He raced back to the farmyard.
A new tyre fitted neatly into his
bucket, and he carried it back
so Tony could be fixed.
Thank you, Tiny!

Read these words again

small

straw

every

trailer

towed

finally

smelly

neatly

tyre

edge

thump

watch

heavy

plough

What can you see here?

hen house

tyre

straw bale

cloud

fields

tractor

Duck in the Dark

In the middle of Sunshine Farm, there was a pond. It was home to a family of ducks. There was Mummy Duck, Daddy Duck, and seven little ducklings. The smallest of them all was called Dandy.

Dandy was a good little duck, and went to sleep early every night like his mummy told him to. He swam into the reeds, tucked his head into his feathers, and closed his eyes.

One day, Dandy couldn't get to sleep. He was getting bigger, and wanted to stay up late like his brothers and sisters. So he kept his eyes open, and peeped out from under his wing.

Things looked very different as night began to fall. The shadows grew long, and loomed at him across the water. Then the sun disappeared, and it became dark and cold. Dandy quacked in dismay.

'Mummy!' he cried. 'The sun has fallen out of the sky!' His mummy swam close and gave him a cuddle. 'Don't worry,' she said. 'It will be back again tomorrow.'

Sure enough, when Dandy woke up the next morning, he could see the sun shining on the water. He poked his bill out from the reeds to check it was in the sky. How lovely to feel its warmth on his feathers!

Read these words again

reeds   sisters

morning   different

family   shadows

early   dismay

night   fallen

feathers   smallest

brothers   tomorrow

What can you see here?

bullrushes

sun

water lilies

duck

pond

69

Candy Cow's Secret

Candy Cow ran across the field as fast as she could. 'Where are you going?' asked Gertie Goat. 'It's a secret,' replied Candy, and carried on running.

Candy ran into the farmyard and towards the stables. 'Where are you going?' crowed Richie Rooster. 'It's a secret,' replied Candy, and sneaked inside the open door.

A little while later, Candy Cow came out of the stables. 'Where have you been?' purred Crystal Cat, sleepily. 'I'm not telling,' said Candy, and ran back through the gate.

All of the farm animals were puzzled. Why was Candy leaving her field each day and going to the stables? They couldn't work it out. So the farm mice decided to follow her and watch.

The next day, when Candy Cow made her way into the stables, the mice ran into the roof to see what happened. They were in for a big surprise!

Candy Cow waited until Jasmine the stablehand arrived with her radio. And then Candy Cow began to dance! She jigged and swayed in time to the music. She was a pretty good moo-ver, you know!

Read these words again

secret	puzzled
music	follow
where	surprise
began	waited
asked	sleepily
carried	leaving
happened	through

What can you see here?

sheep

horse

rooster

cowbell

radio

spade

The Magic Scarecrow

Once upon a time, there was a scarecrow. It stood in a field on Sunnybank Farm, and watched the world go by. But it wasn't just an ordinary scarecrow.
It was magic.

The rabbits that gathered around its feet often wished for juicy clover to eat. And, magically, the field where they lived was full of its sweet pink and white flowers.

The bees in the meadows often wished for their favourite flowers to feed on. When the scarecrow heard their song he smiled, and the hedgerows were filled with glorious blossom.

The farmer often drove past on his tractor and waved to the scarecrow. 'I wish we could have a bumper crop this year,' he said, hopefully. And the scarecrow did his best to help.

The birds often visited the scarecrow and wished for more tasty bugs to nibble on. They munched until they were full on the insects that ate the crops. One day, a crow landed on the scarecrow's arm.

'I wish you would let me eat all the tasty corn in this field,' he cawed. The scarecrow frowned. 'Now that's one thing I just can't allow!' And he cast a spell to make the crow fly far away.

Read these words again

magic	ordinary
world	gathered
sweet	watched
flowers	juicy
drove	heard
insects	favourite
tasty	glorious

What can you see here?

birds

butterfly

rabbit

tractor

crow

bees

A New Adventure

It was a glorious sunny morning, and Toby the Tractor was ready for work bright and early. 'You have a new adventure today,' said Farmer Mike. 'We're off to Sunnybrook Farm to help Farmer Joe.'

Toby was excited. 'Do I need my plough?' he asked. 'Or shall I take the baler?' Farmer Mike smiled as he climbed into the driver's seat. 'You won't need any of those today,' he said.

As they pulled into the long driveway of Sunnybrook Farm, Toby looked around. He was confused. Where were the fields full of corn, waiting to be harvested?

Farmer Mike guided Toby into a yard and hitched up a trailer behind him. But the gate they drove through didn't lead to a muddy field. 'You won't be getting dirty today,' laughed Farmer Mike.

Toby gasped as he saw what was in front of him. There were rows and rows of fruit trees, stretching as far as he could see. He had never seen so many trees in his life!

Toby worked hard all day long, pulling his trailer while the farm workers gathered fruit. It was much more tiring than he thought. But it was great fun working with so many other tractors!

Read these words again

sunny

front

never

dirty

smiled

today

tiring

trailer

fruit

great

muddy

climbed

plough

waiting

What can you see here?

brush

apple tree

wooden box

fork

plough

bucket

93